DIALOGUES OF THE GODS

ADAPTED FROM THE DIALOGUES OF LUCIAN OF SAMOSATA

BAUDELAIRE JONES

Black Box Press
Arlington, TX

Library of Congress Control Number: 2008942603

ISBN 978-0-578-00167-8

First Edition

I

Prometheus. Zeus.

PROMETHEUS

Zeus! Have you come to release me?

ZEUS

Release you?

PROMETHEUS

I think I've suffered enough—don't you?

ZEUS

Hah! You don't know what suffering is! Your chains should be heavier! The whole weight of the Caucasus should be on your back! And instead of one vulture pecking at your liver, you should have a dozen! Two dozen! It's your fault these wretched human creatures have made such a mess of the planet—you stole fire for them, gave them the secrets of invention, and worst of all, you invented women!

PROMETHEUS

I'm surprised you complain about that. You seem to enjoy them well enough.

ZEUS

Oh, women have their uses, I can't deny it, but then I have to listen to them babble on afterwards!

PROMETHEUS

Is it really such a crime that I deserve to feed this damned bird with my liver year after year?

ZEUS

This? You think *this* is bad? Hah! Wait until I get creative!
This is just the beginning!

PROMETHEUS

What if I told you I have valuable information—information I
might trade for my release?

ZEUS

Promethean wiles! What could you possibly tell me that I don't
already know myself?

PROMETHEUS

Have you been blessed with the prophet's eye?

ZEUS

Pfff! You're no prophet!

PROMETHEUS

What if I could tell you the nature of your present errand—
would that convince you?

ZEUS

Maybe. But be specific! Don't try any of your fortune teller
tricks with me!

PROMETHEUS

You're plotting a secret rendezvous with Thetis.

ZEUS

That's right. How did you know? I've got a little something for
her.

PROMETHEUS

Better keep that little something in your pants.

ZEUS

Mind your own business!

PROMETHEUS

Have no intercourse with her, Zeus. If the daughter of Nereus
bears you a son, he will spell your doom.

ZEUS

My "doom?" What the hell does that mean?

PROMETHEUS

He will strike you down and steal your kingdom.

ZEUS

You don't say?

PROMETHEUS

As surely as I'm chained here. The Fates have decreed it.

ZEUS

My whole kingdom, eh?

PROMETHEUS

Avoid any union with Thetis, if you value that thunderbolt of
yours.

ZEUS

Forget her, then—she isn't worth it. She's not the only game in
town. All right, fine—this is valuable information. I'll send
Hephaestus to set you free.

♊

Eros. Zeus.

EROS
Mercy, Zeus! It wasn't very nice of me, but I'm just a child! A wayward child!

ZEUS
A child? Hah! And born before the Titans ruled the Earth! You're a meddling, mean-spirited old man, Eros, and you won't get any mercy from me just because you have no beard or white hair!

EROS
What harm have I ever done that you talk of chaining me in Prometheus' place?

ZEUS
What harm?! Ask your own guilty conscience! You were about to send me off to a tryst with death! That's right, I know all about it! Prometheus spilled the beans on Thetis and the prophecy of *Zeus's doom*! No woman's worth that! Not to mention all the little pranks you've played over the years! Every time you send me down to Earth to have a little fun with some mortal, I have to change into a bull, a satyr, a swan, an eagle … I'm a one-man zoo! I'm surprised you haven't had me turn into a bunny rabbit or a titmouse!

EROS
The logistics of that might be entertaining.

ZEUS
Why can't these women ever be in love with *me?* I am the ruler of Olympus, after all! Why do they always have to have some

sort of animal fixation! Just once, I'd like to show up as myself—be appreciated for my own charms! I mean, what kind of woman does it with a swan?! As long as I'm honking and molting and flapping those ridiculous wings, she's in heaven, but the second I show my true form, she nearly kills herself trying to escape! I don't get it.

EROS
The fault lies not with you, but with these mortal women—the sight of Zeus is too much for them.

ZEUS
Now you're just kissing my ass. Apollo doesn't have this problem. Maybe it's the hair.

EROS
Many mortals are taken with his beautiful hair and smooth chin, but Daphne, at least, was terrified enough to be turned into a tree rather than suffer his advances. Listen, if you really want to win the hearts of these mortal women, I'll tell you what to do. Leave that thunderbolt of yours at home—it's much too loud for love-making.

ZEUS
I think it adds a nice touch.

EROS
Only if you want to scare the maidens out of their minds. Take my advice, make yourself up—curl your hair, tie it up with some ribbon, get a nice purple cloak and some gold-plated shoes, and hire your own personal orchestra to follow you around while courting—make sure to include several flutes—and we'll see if you don't attract an entourage of pretty little love-smitten females. You'll put Dionysus and his Maenads to shame!

ZEUS

Hah! If that's what it takes, you can count me out—you won't make a dandy out of Zeus!

EROS

Fine, then—don't fall in love.

ZEUS

But what else will I do with myself? Maybe I'll have to try a different kind of prey—one that doesn't require flutes and ribbons!

III

Zeus. Hermes.

ZEUS
Hermes! Do you know Io, the daughter of Inachus?

HERMES
Of course.

ZEUS
She's a cow!

HERMES
That's not very nice. I think she's quite lovely.

ZEUS
No, I mean literally—she's a cow.

HERMES
Ah! Sorcery! How did it happen?

ZEUS
Hera! She caught me with the poor girl and transformed her in a
jealous rage! But that isn't all—as if this punishment wasn't
enough, she's charged Argos, a giant with a hundred eyes, to
guard the heifer and keep her at pasture. Io has spent the entire
day eating weeds and swatting flies with her tail!

HERMES
Well, perhaps you should be a little more discreet in your
liaisons.

ZEUS

Spare me the lectures. Just fly down to Nemea and slay the
giant. I'd do it myself, but Hera won't let me out of her sight.
Take Io across the sea to Egypt and set her up there as some
kind of goddess—that way I can visit whenever the mood strikes
me. Tell the Egyptians she has great powers—she can flood the
Nile, regulate the winds, that sort of thing.

HERMES

What shall I call her?

ZEUS

Call her … Isis. That sounds like a good Egyptian name.

HERMES

Isis it is.

IV

Zeus. Ganymede.

ZEUS

Well, Ganymede, here we are. Mount Olympus!

GANYMEDE

What happened to your crooked beak and your sharp talons?
Where are your wings?

ZEUS

Don't you like me much better this way? Why don't you give
me a kiss?

GANYMEDE

So you're just a man? You're not an eagle after all? Why did
you carry me off from my flock?

ZEUS

So many questions! I only appeared to you in the semblance of
a bird, dear boy, so that I might carry you here—to the home of
the gods.

GANYMEDE

Are you a god?

ZEUS

Of course—the greatest of them all.

GANYMEDE

But how can you be the great Pan when you haven't a syrinx or
horns or even hairy legs?

ZEUS

Hah! Do you really think Pan is the greatest of the gods?

GANYMEDE

I don't know. Father sacrifices a he-goat to him every year. But you don't look anything like Pan. I think you're just some kidnapping slave-dealer or other.

ZEUS

Tell me, boy, have you never heard the name of Zeus?

GANYMEDE

Zeus the Rain-Sender? The Thunderer?

ZEUS

That's right.

GANYMEDE

If you're Zeus, what sin has caused you to carry me away from my flock and my family? Even now, the wolves must be feasting on my defenseless sheep.

ZEUS

What do you care for sheep and family now that you live with the gods?! You're immortal now!

GANYMEDE

What do you mean? You ... you aren't going to take me home to Ida?

ZEUS

No. That would be a lot of wasted effort, wouldn't it—changing to an eagle and all that for no reason?

GANYMEDE

My father won't like this. He'll be looking for me, and when he finds me, I'll be whipped for leaving my flock.

ZEUS

How will he ever find you here?

GANYMEDE

I don't want to stay here! Please! I already miss him! And my mother! Take me back, and I promise to sacrifice our new ram as my ransom! He's a three-year-old! A fine animal who leads the flock to pasture!

ZEUS

How simple and innocent you are, my dear Ganymede. It's a refreshing change from the lot I usually deal with. But you mustn't hold on to the past. Forget all those earthly things—the flock, Ida, your earthly parents—you're one of us now, a celestial being. It will be a great credit to your father and your country to have produced such a being; and instead of cheese and milk, you will feast on ambrosia and nectar! In fact, this latter is the reason I brought you here—your job will be to pour nectar for the gods! You will be our cupbearer! For this simple service, you will become immortal and you shall be happy for all eternity!

GANYMEDE

But who will play with me?

ZEUS

I'm sure young Eros would be delighted to entertain you.

GANYMEDE

Is he about my age?

ZEUS

Somewhere thereabouts.

GANYMEDE

Why do you need me to pour your nectar? How hard can it be?
Any fool can pass the milk-bowl.

ZEUS

There you go again, thinking in terms of earthly things. This is
no milk we drink here, but celestial nectar.

GANYMEDE

Is it sweeter than milk?

ZEUS

You'll find out for yourself soon enough—once you've tasted it,
you'll never be able to stomach milk again!

GANYMEDE

Where will I sleep? With this other boy, Eros?

ZEUS

No. That's why I brought you here—don't you want to share
my bed?

GANYMEDE

Why would I want to do that?

ZEUS

Because I desire it. Sleep would be so much more pleasant if I
had you to look at, beautiful boy.

GANYMEDE

How would looking at me help you sleep?

ZEUS

You have a certain sweet charm that might bring it on more easily.

GANYMEDE

My mother and father were always annoyed when I slept in the same bed with him. They used to complain that I spent the whole night kicking and talking in my sleep. If that's really why you brought me here, you should probably fly me back down to Earth again, or else I'll keep you awake all night with my tossing and turning.

ZEUS

A little thrashing about might please me—since I plan to keep you awake with a thousand kisses.

GANYMEDE

What? I'm not interested in that, thank you—I'd rather sleep.

ZEUS

There's plenty of time to see about that after you taste immortality. For now, go find Hermes. Tell him you are to be our cup-bearer, and he will instruct you on the finer points of handling the cup.

V

Hera. Zeus.

                    HERA
Zeus! We need to talk!

                    ZEUS
Oh god.

                    HERA
You haven't looked at me once since that Phrygian boy came
into our home.

                    ZEUS
What—are you jealous?

                    HERA
Maybe.

                    ZEUS
Why don't you turn him into a cow?

                    HERA
Don't tempt me!

                    ZEUS
I thought you were only concerned about women I happen to be
intimate with?

                    HERA
He's just a boy! How can you—

ZEUS

Oh, this whole thing with Ganymede is completely innocent. I
don't know why you're making such a big fuss.

HERA

You should be ashamed of yourself! Lord of the gods! Hah!
Your behavior wouldn't be proper even if you were some mortal
peasant! You desert me, your lawful wife, and go carousing
with mortal women at all hours of the day and night with no
consideration for my feelings! It's not respectable!

ZEUS

Respectable? Hah!

HERA

But at least those sluts of yours remained on Earth, while you've
brought this youth from Ida into my own house! He actually
lives with us! I have to pick up after him!

ZEUS

As if you've ever done any housekeeping in your life!

HERA

How would you know?! You don't pay any attention to me!
It's like I don't exist!

ZEUS

I don't know how you can say you don't exist—you've certainly
grown large enough.

HERA

Oh!

ZEUS

It's no wonder you want to turn all my lovers into heifers—
that's the only way you can compete!

HERA

If I've taken refuge in food and wine, it's because my husband
would rather fondle the cup-bearer than his own wife!

ZEUS

Why do you persist in these absurd accusations?

HERA

Oh, I've seen how you take the cup from him! Everyone sees!
It's embarrassing! Even when you're not thirsty! After tasting,
you hand the cup back and insist that he drink too, then you
receive it again, all googly-eyed, making sure to take the
remainder from the spot where the boy has placed his lips so you
can drink and kiss at the same time in front of us all! Do you
really think we're so dim-witted that we can't see it?! And this
morning, I actually witnessed you, the King and father of the
universe, with that big beard you've grown, lay aside your aegis
and thunderbolt to play a game of marbles with the boy! You'll
take any excuse to get close to him, and don't think that I don't
see it!

ZEUS

I'm not allowed to play marbles now?

HERA

It's not the marbles I object to, but all the kissing during the
game!

ZEUS

Is it really such an awful crime to kiss a fair youth? Believe me,
Hera, should I allow him to kiss you even once, you would
understand why I prefer his innocent kiss to yours!

HERA

Zeus, King of the Gods—a pedophile and a degenerate!

ZEUS

Oh, stop making everything so dramatic. Do you really want
that son of yours, Hephaestus, to carry our drinks, with that
embarrassing limp of his and coming straight from the forge as
he does, dripping sweat everywhere and all covered with soot?
Not even you, his own mother, could kiss that face with
pleasure! No, whether you admit it or not, the present
arrangement is much more agreeable for everyone. Ganymede
is clean and rosy-fingered and hands the goblet deftly.

HERA

Yes. Hephaestus is deformed now, and his fingers aren't fit to
touch your cup, and the sight of him makes you sick—but you
never noticed any of these things until your sights fell on this
boy from Ida. It certainly didn't prevent you from drinking prior
to his arrival.

ZEUS

Your jealousy only intensifies my love for him. If you don't
appreciate receiving the goblet from a beautiful boy, let that son
of yours pour your wine—I'll keep Ganymede for myself.
     [Enter GANYMEDE in tears.]
What's this? In tears? Don't worry, child—if anyone has any
intention of harming you, they will have Zeus to answer to.

VI

Hera. Zeus.

HERA

What do you think of this man—Ixion?

ZEUS

Why? Are you contemplating an affair? I think you should do it—he's a fine sort.

HERA

He is not! He's a villain!

ZEUS

I'm intrigued by this little outburst. Is there something going on I should know about?

HERA

There most certainly is!

ZEUS

Well? Go on—the anticipation is killing me!

HERA

You don't have to make fun. It's hard enough for me to tell you as it is. The wretch!

ZEUS

Ah! If he's a "wretch," you must certainly tell me all about it. I know what "wretch" means on your prudish tongue. Who has he been making love to?

HERA

Me!

ZEUS

You? Really? And he seemed so sensible.

HERA

It's been going on for a long time. At first, I noticed him
staring—out of the corner of his eye, you know, but glancing
away when I caught him—then he started in with the sighs and
groans.

ZEUS

Maybe he was constipated.

HERA

I'll ignore that little remark. I wasn't sure either, at first, but
whenever I hand my cup to Ganymede, he insists on having it
next and slobbers all over it, kissing more than drinking, and
lifting his eyes to me again, and that's when I knew. I would
have told you then and there, but I thought his mad fit might
pass. It did not, however, and today he has crossed the line—he
actually dared to speak to me!

ZEUS

Speak to you?

HERA

Yes!

ZEUS

Ah! So you haven't actually *made love* yet?

HERA

I left him weeping and groveling at my feet. I stopped my ears
so as not to hear his impertinences, and came directly to you. It
is for you to determine his punishment.

ZEUS

Wow! I have a rival—and with my own wife! Fascinating!
Here is a rascal who has tippled nectar to some purpose! Well,
we have no one to blame but ourselves. We admit these mortals
to our table, share the celestial nectar, parade before them all the
beauties of Heaven—is it any wonder that they fall in love and
form ambitious schemes? Love is all-powerful, after all, and not
just for mortals—we Gods have sometimes fallen victim to his
potent darts.

HERA

You're certainly a chronic case, eternally under his sway.
You're like a little toy, Love's pawn, he leads you about by the
nose, and you assume every shape at his command. I know very
well how this will end—you're going to pardon Ixion because
you've had relations with his wife and turnabout is fair play.

ZEUS

Ah! I'd forgotten all about her—you have a better memory for
these little outings of mine than I have!

HERA

Stop reminiscing about your adventures and tell me what you
plan to do about Ixion.

ZEUS

Well, it would never to do banish him—that would just cause a
scandal. No, since he's so fond of you, perhaps we should just
satisfy his appetite, you know—allow him to glut himself on this
strange desire.

HERA

What?! You want me to open my legs for this mortal?!

ZEUS

No, no, of course not—believe it or not, you still have a few
charms left, and I'd like to keep you for myself. I was thinking
we could make a cloud-phantom in your image, and after dinner,
you know, as he lies awake dreaming of you and vainly striving
to soothe his desire, we'll lay this phantom-lady at his side.
He'll think you've come to satisfy him, and the conquest
complete, he'll move on to a more willing victim.

HERA

Never! The presumptuous devil!

ZEUS

What harm can it do if Ixion makes love to a cloud?

HERA

He will think *I* am the cloud and that he's working his wicked
little will on *me!*

ZEUS

Oh, don't be ridiculous. The cloud is not Hera, and Hera is not
the cloud. It's just an illusion. He might as well be doing
himself.

HERA

While he's thinking of me!

ZEUS

You don't think that's happened already?

HERA

You men are all alike! What if he goes home afterwards and
brags about how he's made Hera scream like a little girl, and
made a cuckold of Zeus in the bargain—that won't bother you?

ZEUS

If he says anything of the kind, I'll plant my thunderbolt so far up his … well, somewhere that won't be very comfortable for him! And it'll serve him right! Not for falling in love—I see no great harm in that—but for letting his tongue wag.

VII

Hephaestus. Apollo.

HEPHAESTUS
Apollo! Have you seen Maia's baby? Oh, what a treasure!
Such a pretty little thing, and such a sweet smile!

APOLLO
That baby's no treasure—it's a mischievous little imp!

HEPHAESTUS
What harm could that sweet baby do—he was only just born?

APOLLO
Ask Poseidon; it stole his trident.

HEPHAESTUS
No!

APOLLO
Yes.

HEPHAESTUS
I'm sure it was just an innocent mistake.

APOLLO
Ares just informed me that his sword was stolen as well—right
out of the scabbard.

HEPHAESTUS
Really?

APOLLO

And that's not all—my bow and arrows have gone missing as well, not two minutes after I made the mistake of petting that infant's abominable little head.

HEPHAESTUS

You must be mistaken! He's just a baby—he can barely even walk!

APOLLO

You'll find out for yourself, Hephaestus, if he gets within reach of you.

HEPHAESTUS

He has been.

APOLLO

And are all of your tools accounted for?

HEPHAESTUS

Of course.

APOLLO

Nothing's missing?

HEPHAESTUS

Not that I know of.

APOLLO

I advise you to make sure.

HEPHAESTUS

Zeus! Where are my pincers?

APOLLO

You will find them in his diapers.

HEPHAESTUS
He's a light-fingered little tramp!

APOLLO
Yes, I'd swear he's practiced petty larceny in the womb.
Yesterday he challenged Eros to a wrestling match—

HEPHAESTUS
But even little Eros is twice his size!

APOLLO
Size, apparently, is no obstacle. He tripped up his heels
somehow and had him on his back in a twinkling. Before the
applause could die down, he had pressed Aphrodite for a
congratulatory hug and stolen her girdle. Zeus hadn't finished
laughing before his scepter was gone as well. Thank goodness
the thunderbolt is too heavy or he would have made off with that
too!

HEPHAESTUS
Well, the child has some spirit, I'd say.

APOLLO
Spirit, yes—there's no doubt about that. And some musical
ability as well.

HEPHAESTUS
Musical ability—at his age?

APOLLO
I'll say.

HEPHAESTUS
Do you mean to say he can actually play an instrument?

APOLLO

An instrument of his own making! He found a dead tortoise lying on the road somewhere and fitted horns to it, a cross-bar, stuck in pegs, inserted a bridge, and started in playing a melancholy old tune so skillfully and with such passion that it made an old musician like me quite green with envy. Even at night, Maia says he won't keep still, poking his nose into Hades—on some thieves' errand, no doubt.

HEPHAESTUS

No doubt.

APOLLO

Well, you'd better go retrieve your pincers before Hermes soils his diaper and dirties your instrument.

HEPHAESTUS

If I see your arrows, I'll let you know.

VIII

Hephaestus. Zeus.

HEPHAESTUS

Zeus! You sent for me? Here I am—and with an axe so sharp it could cleave a stone at one blow!

ZEUS

Yes! Thank god you're here, Hephaestus! Just split my head in half, will you?

HEPHAESTUS

Is this some sort of joke?

ZEUS

No!

HEPHAESTUS

You … you can't seriously expect me to—

ZEUS

Crack my skull! Do it! If you give me any lip, I'll chain you to the Caucasus!

HEPHAESTUS

But … I … I—

ZEUS

Stop stuttering and do what I say! A good lusty stroke—right here! I'm in the pangs of childbirth and need some relief!

HEPHAESTUS

I'll follow your instructions, but understand the axe is sharp and will prove a rough midwife.

29

ZEUS

Hew away and fear nothing! My brain is in a whirl, but I know
what I'm doing!

HEPHAESTUS

All right, here goes nothing.
[He strikes.]
Well, what have we here? A maiden—and in full armor too!
It's a wonder you had room for any thoughts at all with this full-
grown woman dancing around your head! And what a headache
you must have had if she was this active in the "womb!" It must
be some sort of war dance, the way she's whipping that spear
and shield about! It's inspired! And she's so ... bouncy! Those
grey eyes! Not many women look so fetching under a war
helmet! Zeus, as the fee for my midwifery, I claim her hand in
marriage!

ZEUS

Impossible! Not that I have any personal objection to your
request, but Athena—that's the girl's name—is obstinate. She's
determined to remain a virgin.

HEPHAESTUS

I'll accept nothing else.

ZEUS

All right, fine—if you can carry her off, she's yours. But it may
be easier said than done!

IX

Poseidon. Hermes.

POSEIDON
Hermes! Can you get me in to see Zeus?

HERMES
I'm sorry, Poseidon—this isn't a good time.

POSEIDON
Can't you pull a few strings?

HERMES
Not now. He's … indisposed at the moment.

POSEIDON
Ah—"engaged" with Hera, is he?

HERMES
No ... not exactly.

POSEIDON
I see. He must be "closeted" with Ganymede then.

HERMES
Not that, either. It's difficult to explain, but … he's not feeling
well.

POSEIDON
Did he catch some sort of STD? He really ought to be more
careful with those mortal women.

HERMES
No, you're on the wrong track, uncle.

31

POSEIDON

Why don't you just tell me—you know I can be trusted.

HERMES

All right, but you can't tell anyone. He's been put on bed rest.

POSEIDON

For what? Is it serious?

HERMES

No, he's ... with child.

POSEIDON

With child? Get out of here! Is this one of your practical jokes?

HERMES

Do I look like I'm joking?

POSEIDON

But how? By whom? Who's the father? Is he a hermaphrodite?
And without us knowing it all this time!

HERMES

No, no, it's not like that. I mean, it's not the usual part that
holds the embryo.

POSEIDON

Ah! I see—he's given birth again through his cranium! Like he
did with Athena. What a fertile mind he has!

HERMES

No, it was his thigh this time.

POSEIDON

He's productive all over! Every part of his body! But who was
his partner in this affair?

HERMES

Semele, a lady of Thebes, one of the daughters of Cadmus. He
paid her a visit and impregnated her.

POSEIDON

Then did he take her place in the straw?

HERMES

I know it must seem very strange. But Hera—you know how
jealous she is—she laid a trap for the poor woman and
convinced her to ask Zeus to come equipped with thunder and
lightning for their union. Zeus was only too happy to oblige—
he's used to taking the shape of any number of animals, so when
she asked him to come as himself, he was delighted. But his
thunderbolt set the roof on fire, the whole house went up in
flames, and his mistress died a horrible death. I cut the infant
from the lady's womb just in time, it was still alive, but barely—
a still imperfect embryo. There was nowhere else to put it so
Zeus sliced open his own thigh and inserted the youngling so it
could survive until birth. But the pregnancy hasn't been easy
and he isn't feeling well.

POSEIDON

That's quite a story. Has he thought of any names?

HERMES

He's going to name the child Dionysus and plans to let the
Nymphs raise him as their own.

POSEIDON

So in a way, he really is both father and mother to this
Dionysus?

HERMES

So it seems. Anyway, I'm off to fetch chocolate and cheese—
I've never seen him eat this much—and to perform certain other
services which are customary under such circumstances.

POSEIDON

He hasn't asked you to rub his feet, has he?

HERMES

Oh, I knew I shouldn't have told you.

X

Hermes. Helios.

HERMES
Helios, you are to cancel your drive today, and tomorrow as well—Zeus's orders.

HELIOS
These are strange instructions, Hermes.

HERMES
You are to remain at home for the duration and let this interval of time be like one long night. I'll have the Horae unharness your horses and put out your fires. Just consider this a little vacation.

HELIOS
Have I done something wrong?

HERMES
No, not at all.

HELIOS
Did I blunder my course in some way or drive beyond my bounds?

HERMES
Don't take it so personally.

HELIOS
I must have done something wrong for Zeus to make the night three times the length of one day.

HERMES

No, you don't understand. It's only temporary. He wants to prolong this particular night for certain business he has to attend to.

HELIOS

What sort of business?

HERMES

The usual sort. He's making love to Amphitryon's wife.

HELIOS

And one night isn't enough?

HERMES

Apparently not. According to Zeus, some mighty divinity is to be born from this intercourse, and it's simply not possible for him to be turned out complete and perfect in a single night.

HELIOS

Well, I wish him luck in this endeavor, but this sort of thing was not the fashion in the time of Cronos. In those days, a day was a day, and a night was a night, and a King of the Gods was expected to keep his own wife company in the darkness of the night, according to its proper measure and proportionate to its hours. Now, everything is strange and confused. Cronos wouldn't have been caught dead with a mortal woman—they were beneath him. But Zeus would have us turn everything upside down for the benefit of some wretched female, and my horses will become unmanageable from want of work, and the route of the sun, by remaining untrodden for three successive days, will become almost impassable. Men will pass the time miserably in the darkness and the whole planet will come to a standstill, while Zeus works away on his mistress, pumping out this fine hero you speak of. I hope he's worth it.

HERMES

Watch your tongue, Helios, or you may pay a heavy price for those angry words. I must be off to Selene and Hypnus, Zeus has instructions for them as well—that the former may be leisurely in her journey, and that the latter may hold tight to mortals, that they may not realize the night has been so long.

XI

Aphrodite. Selene.

APHRODITE

So what's this I hear, Selene—that you've taken to pausing the moon in the sky every night so you can gaze like a schoolgirl at this hunter, Endymion, while he sleeps?

SELENE

Who told you that?

APHRODITE

Oh, I have my sources. Sometimes, they say, you actually abandon your post and join him in his bed. Is this true?

SELENE

Ask that son of yours—it's his fault.

APHRODITE

Ah! Such a naughty boy, my son! He plays the same wicked games on his own mother, you know! First he smites me with an insatiable desire for Anchises of Troy, then before I can get my fill of that noble prince, he redirects my love pangs toward some Assyrian stripling or some Phoenician farm boy, and I'm off for Lebanon, Cyprus, Tripoli, like some crazed bitch in heat! It makes me dizzy! I can't catch my breath! And worse, once I'm smitten, he doesn't even leave the man to me, but makes some other goddess or mortal beauty in love with him as well, so that half the time I don't get any satisfaction at all! It makes me so mad, I want to strangle the little devil! I've threatened to clip his wings and break all of his arrows—I've spanked his little bottom until I was blue in the face! He cries for a minute or two, promises never to do it again, and two seconds later he's back to his games. But enough about me! I want to know about

38

your new lover, Endymion! Is he handsome? Does he have fine, broad shoulders and a chiseled torso? That's always a consolation in our humiliation—to have a strapping young warrior aroused to distraction by our charms. It certainly doesn't hurt one's ego.

SELENE

Oh, he's handsome all right. You should see him asleep on the rock, his javelin still resting in his left hand, the right arm bent upwards, framing his beautiful face. I creep noiselessly to him, treading on tiptoe, and lie so close that his soft breath kisses my face, but I'm afraid to wake him … I'm dying of love, Aphrodite. But I don't have to tell you—you understand.

XII

Aphrodite. Eros.

APHRODITE

Child, you must think before you act. It's bad enough the way
you toy with mortals down there—always inciting them to some
mischief or another, and always in the name of love—but to play
such games with the immortal Gods … that's a much more
dangerous proposal. You morph Zeus into whatever shape you
like, as if he were some changeling made for your amusement;
you lure Selene down from the sky where she belongs; you force
Helios to linger with Clymene until it is almost too late for him
to drive out at all! And I won't even mention the naughty tricks
you play on your own mother! Of course, you know you're safe
there—I could never harm my darling little Eros—but Rhea?!
How could you even think of sending her after that Phrygian
fellow?! A woman of her age! And mother of so many Gods!
She's completely lost her senses—she harnesses those lions of
hers and dashes all over Ida in some sort of Bacchic frenzy with
the Corybantes, shrieking for Attis here and there, slashing her
arms and rushing over the hills like a wild thing with disheveled
hair! It isn't proper! Listen to me, one of these days when she
is in a mad fit—or perhaps when she finally comes to her
senses—she will send the Corybantes after you, my child, with
orders to tear you apart and throw you to the lions!

EROS

It's all right, mother. I'm not afraid of lions. I like them. I like
to ride on their backs and hold on to their manes, and when I put
my hand in their mouths, they only lick it. And besides, what's
so bad about making people fall in love? Isn't love beautiful?
How would you feel if Ares suddenly stopped loving you?

40

APHRODITE

Oh, my beautiful boy! How can I answer that? But someday you will remember what I've said, and you will understand that mother was right.

XIII

Zeus. Asclepius. Heracles.

ZEUS
Enough fighting, you two! You might as well act like grown men. Your behavior isn't appropriate for the table of the Gods.

HERACLES
Is this *pharmacist* really to have a higher place than me?

ASCLEPIUS
Of course—I'm your better.

HERACLES
You pompous fool! It was Zeus's thunderbolt that cracked your skull for your unholy doings, and he's only granted you immortality again out of sheer pity!

ASCLEPIUS
I seem to remember some other god who was burnt to death—on Mount Oeta, was it?

HERACLES
Don't compare my life to yours. It isn't the same at all. Everyone knows how I toiled away for years, cleansing the earth of monsters and punishing vile men. What have you ever done besides robbing graves and using your medical prowess for monetary gain? You've never shown an ounce of real courage in your life!

ASCLEPIUS
Do you really stand here and accuse me—you, whose wounds I healed not long ago when you crawled up here all burnt like a piece of toast?!

HERACLES

I do!

ASCLEPIUS

At least I was never a slave! And I never killed my own wife in a fit of rage!

HERACLES

That's it! I'll teach you a lesson or two! Immortality won't do you much good when I've broken every bone in your body and ground you to ashes!

ZEUS

Enough! Stop your childish bickering and shake hands, or I'll send you both away from the table without any food! Heracles, Asclepius died before you and therefore has the right to a better place. End of discussion.

XIV

Hermes. Apollo.

HERMES
What's wrong, Apollo? Why so sad?

APOLLO
Oh, my love!

HERMES
Ah! Still brooding over that affair with Daphne?

APOLLO
No. I grieve for my beloved Hyacinth, the son of Oebalus.

HERMES
Hyacinth? He's not dead.

APOLLO
He is.

HERMES
Who killed him? What kind of monster could raise a hand to that lovely boy!

APOLLO
I did.

HERMES
What?! You must have been mad!

APOLLO
No; it was an accident.

HERMES

Apollo ... I'm so sorry. How did it happen?

APOLLO

He wanted to learn how to throw the discus. He'd been begging
me for weeks, so I finally took him out to the field. We were
throwing, and I ... I had just sent my discus high into the air
when jealous Zephyr—cursed be he above all winds—came out
of nowhere and dashed the discus down upon the child's head.
His beautiful head cracked like a melon ... blood everywhere ...
it was all over in an instant.

HERMES

I knew the boy had spurned Zephyr's advances, but this ...

APOLLO

I buried Hyacinth at the very spot where he fell, and from his
blood I have made a flower to spring up, the sweetest and fairest
of all flowers, inscribed with the letters of woe. As for Zephyr, I
will sharpen my arrows and pursue him to the ends of the earth.
He will pay dearly for his actions.

HERMES

Let it go, Apollo. Your grief is unreasonable.

APOLLO

Unreasonable?! How can you—

HERMES

You knew that your heart was set upon a mortal—didn't you?

APOLLO

Of course.

HERMES

Then how then can you grieve for his mortality?

XV

Hermes. Apollo.

HERMES
It just isn't fair! A cripple like him?

APOLLO
I know.

HERMES
I mean, how does he deserve two beauties such as Aphrodite and Charis?!

APOLLO
Luck, my friend. Pure dumb luck.

HERMES
It just seems so strange!

APOLLO
It does—the way they cuddle and kiss him, all sooty-faced and sweaty after hours over the forge.

HERMES
I'm so jealous I may actually burst! I mean, here you are with your long hair and your harp, I'm a decent-looking fellow with some musical ability myself, but when it comes time to turn out the lights, we lie alone while he—

APOLLO
I've had a few lovers.

HERMES
Yes, but it never works out very well—does it?

APOLLO

What do you mean?

HERMES

Daphne turned herself into a tree to escape your love-making!

APOLLO

Well *that* one, sure—

HERMES

And your other great love, you killed with a discus.

APOLLO

All right, all right, I concede the point!

HERMES

It's unfair, that's all I'm saying.

APOLLO

I think I'll go kill myself now.

HERMES

Oh, don't start moping—my love life isn't any better. I mean, I had Aphrodite once, sure, but it was so brief and passing I could hardly enjoy it even in the moment, and here this dirty blacksmith has *two* such beauties, and for as long as he likes!

APOLLO

I don't understand why Aphrodite and Charis aren't jealous of each other.

HERMES

Well, one is his wife on Earth and the other in Heaven.

APOLLO

That's a clever setup.

HERMES

Plus everyone knows Aphrodite's screwing Ares on the side, so she can't really complain about Charis—can she?

APOLLO

Do you think Hephaestus knows?

HERMES

Oh, sure.

APOLLO

And he just accepts it?

HERMES

What's he going to do—challenge Ares to a fight?

APOLLO

Hah! That'd be something!

HERMES

He'd get slaughtered! Although I did hear him bragging about some new invention he's working on—some kind of net, you know, to catch them in the act.

APOLLO

I wouldn't mind being caught in that act.

HERMES

Are you serious? Imagine the humiliation!

APOLLO

I little humiliation is a small price to pay for love.

XVI

Hera. Leto.

HERA

I must congratulate you, madam, on the brood of children
you've provided Zeus. He must be tickled pink—you've been
very *productive*.

LETO

We can't all be the proud mothers of Hephaestuses.

HERA

My son may be a cripple, but at least he's of some use! He's a
master blacksmith, and he's made Heaven a fine place to live!
Aphrodite thought him worth marrying! What about those two
of yours? The girl is completely out of control and, well,
mannish!

LETO

Watch what you say about Artemis.

HERA

Her behavior in Scythia reflects badly on all of us. I mean,
really—butchering strangers and eating them?! You must be so
proud. And Apollo, well, he certainly pretends to be clever,
with his oracles and his prophecies, but I've never heard such a
bunch of nonsense. His answers are always so vague and
ambiguous that one way or another he can claim he was right,
but who can make any sense of them until after the fact? He's a
cheat, that's all. A fake. But there are plenty of fools out there
willing to part with their money for a palm reading.

LETO

Just because *you* don't understand his prophecies—

HERA

This *prophet* of yours couldn't even foresee that he was going to kill his favorite with a discus! Hah! And did he predict that Daphne would run away in terror, as handsome as he is, with his long, flowing hair?! I'm not sure which is worse—the phony prophet or the cannibalistic barbarian!

LETO

Fine. My children are butchers and impostors. I know how you hate to look at them. I watch you practically boil over with rage every time someone compliments Artemis on her looks or admires Apollo's music.

HERA

His *music?* Excuse a smile, but if the Muses hadn't shown such favoritism in that little contest with Marsyas, your son would have lost his skin on account of his *music*. As for your charming daughter, I think there may be a good reason she refuses to let any man examine her too closely. I mean, when Actaeon caught a glimpse of her naked, she had his own dogs tear him apart to keep him quiet. What is she hiding? Something hideous, I suspect.

LETO

I hope you're enjoying this moment. I hope you're having a good time. You are the legal wife of Zeus and share his throne, so you may insult whomever you please. But it's only a matter of time before he seeks comfort in some other woman's bed, as we both know he has done so many times before, and then, madam, there will be tears—I don't need Apollo to tell me that.

XVII

Apollo. Hermes.

APOLLO

What's so funny, Hermes? Why are you laughing?

HERMES

I've just seen the most ridiculous sight!

APOLLO

Tell me—what was it?

HERMES

Aphrodite and Ares! Hephaestus caught them in the act! And
he's preserved them like flies in amber!

APOLLO

How? What did he do?

HERMES

Well, as we suspected, he's been aware of their affair for quite
some time, and he's been stalking them like prey—laying a
clever trap. This morning, he planted invisible fetters in their
bed, then went to work in the forge as usual. When Ares and
Aphrodite made use of the bed, they soon found themselves
entangled in more than each other's arms! The more they
squirmed, the tighter this invisible net held them! Then
Hephaestus storms in! They had no chance to hide their shame,
completely naked and exposed as they were! At first, Ares
hurled a few useless threats and tried to break his bonds, but
realizing his efforts were useless, he began to act the suppliant.

APOLLO

What did Hephaestus do then? Did he release them?

HERMES

Oh, no! He summoned all the Gods to see his little peepshow!

APOLLO

Really?

HERMES

He wants the two lovers to feel the full weight of their shame.
You should see the two of them, eyes fixed on the ground and
blushing, but still trapped in their love pose! They're both very
athletic—I'll give them that much.

APOLLO

Have I missed it?

HERMES

Not at all. I suspect he'll be selling tickets all day.

APOLLO

But doesn't Hephaestus feel a bit embarrassed himself exposing
this affair—I mean, it is his wife, after all.

HERMES

No, he can't stop laughing. But I have to be honest, you were
right—I grudge Ares not only his relations with the fairest of the
Goddesses, but even his being bound with her.

APOLLO

I told you.

HERMES

But quick, come and have a look before Hephaestus comes to
his senses. You don't want to miss this!

XVIII

Hera. Zeus.

HERA
Well, I would be ashamed to show my face in public if *I* had a son like that—so effeminate, tying ribbons in his hair and dancing around with mad women all the time. He's practically a woman himself—he resembles any one of them more than his father.

ZEUS
This effeminate wearer of ribbons, as you call him, has conquered Lydia, subdued Thrace, enslaved the people of Tmolus, not to mention leading his female host on an expedition all the way to India where he took possession of that country and put its king in chains.

HERA
And he never stopped dancing the whole time—never relinquished the thyrsus or the wine cup!

ZEUS
If you ask me, that's quite an accomplishment—to do all that in a drunken frenzy.

HERA
He's a sot!

ZEUS
He's inspired. And he doesn't suffer scoffers lightly. If any man mocks him, they are soon mistaken for a fawn by their own mother and torn limb from limb. Are these not the actions of a strong man, a worthy son of Zeus? He's fond of his comforts, there's no doubt about that, and his amusements too—but aren't

we all? If he can achieve all of these things while drunk, imagine how unstoppable Dionysus would be if he were ever sober!

XIX

Aphrodite. Eros.

APHRODITE
Eros, dear, I have a bone to pick with you.

EROS
What is it, mother?

APHRODITE
You've conquered most of the Gods with those arrows of yours—Zeus, Poseidon, Rhea, Apollo, even your own mother … so how is it that you show mercy to Athena? You haven't even tried with her.

EROS
I am afraid of her—the way those awful eyes of hers flash! Every time I point my bow in her direction, she tosses her head and gives me this dark look so that my hand begins to shake and I drop my arrow.

APHRODITE
I should think Ares would be more frightening than her—but you pierced his heart easily enough.

EROS
Yes, but Ares is happy to have me; he relishes my little stings. Athena doesn't want anything to do with me. Once, when I flew too close to her, quite innocently, with my torch, she threatened to run me through with her spear and drop me into Tartarus! There was more, but I can't repeat it—it makes me shake to even think about her threats. I keep seeing that horrible face with the snaky hair that she wears on her breast … it gives me nightmares. No, when I see Athena coming, I run the other way.

APHRODITE

This doesn't make any sense—you're afraid of Athena and the Gorgon, but you laugh at Zeus' thunderbolt? And what about the Muses—why do they get off scot free?

EROS

When I see the Muses, I forget all about my arrows. I love to sit and listen to their music.

APHRODITE

Perhaps I should learn to play the harp—It might have spared me this latest humiliation! But what about Artemis, you never take a shot at her?

EROS

I can't catch her. She always sees me coming and disappears over the hills. Besides, her heart is already engaged.

APHRODITE

Is it? To whom?

EROS

To hunting. She can think of nothing but the hot pursuit of stags and fawns. Her brother, now, he is an archer too—

APHRODITE

I know, child, you've certainly hit *him* often enough.

XX

Zeus. Hermes. Hera. Athena. Aphrodite. Paris.

ZEUS

Hermes, I have an important task for you. Take this apple to
Phrygia. On the Gargaran peak of Ida, you will find a young
herdsman—Paris, the son of Priam. Tell him that he's been
chosen by Zeus to judge the beauty of the Goddesses and to
decide once and for all which one is the most beautiful.

HERMES

What's the apple for?

ZEUS

Oh, that's the prize—for the winner.

HERMES

That's the best you could do?

ZEUS

It's an apple from the table of Zeus! Besides, it's not the prize
that's important, but the honor of being chosen most beautiful of
all the Goddesses. As for myself, I'll have nothing to do with it.
I love you all equally, and if I had my way, all three would win.
But of course one of you has to be honored above the others or
you'll never be satisfied, and if I choose one of you, the other
two will make my life miserable. This young Phrygian, on the
other hand, has an objective eye. Although there is royal blood
in his veins, he is a simple countryman, so he knows what's
what, and he won't play any games.

APHRODITE

It doesn't matter who the judge is. Momus himself can be the
judge, as far as I'm concerned. I have nothing to hide. I mean,
what fault could he possibly find with me? Of course, the others
must agree too.

HERA

Oh, we're not afraid to measure ourselves against you, even if
your lover Ares should be appointed. Paris will do—whoever he
is.

ZEUS

And my little Athena—does she approve? No, no, don't blush
or hide your pretty face. I know it's a delicate subject, but—
there, she nods her consent. Very well, then—it's decided. And
remember, the losers in this contest mustn't be angry with the
judge. I won't have the poor boy punished for his decision.
Only one can wear the crown of beauty.

HERMES

All right, then—we're off to Phrygia. Just follow me, ladies,
and don't be nervous. I know Paris—he's a good boy, quite the
charmer, and a clever judge of beauty. He'll make the right
choice, you can count on it.

APHRODITE

I'm glad you approve of Paris; I ask for nothing but a fair judge.
Do you know if he has a wife, Hermes? Or is he a bachelor?

HERMES

He's not a bachelor in the strictest sense.

APHRODITE

What does that mean?

HERMES
Well, there's a wife ... and she's nice enough ... but she really doesn't deserve him.

APHRODITE
Why not?

HERMES
Well ... she's a "country beauty." In other words, she's downright ugly and he only took her because there was nothing else available, and a young man must have *somewhere* to sow his seed. Why do you ask?

APHRODITE
Just curious.

ATHENA
What's all this whispering about? That isn't fair, Hermes. Whatever you're telling Aphrodite, you can tell the rest of us.

HERMES
It's nothing important. She only asked if Paris was a bachelor.

HERA
None of her business—that's what you should have said.

HERMES
It's an innocent enough question.

ATHENA
Well—is he?

HERMES
A bachelor? No.

ATHENA

What are his ambitions? Does he care for military glory? Or
just for his goats?

HERMES

Well, I don't really know, but he's a young man, so I would
assume he's dreamed of distinction on the battlefield.

APHRODITE

There, you see—*I* don't complain when you whisper to her.

HERMES

Listen, ladies, don't be cross with me; I'm just the messenger.
And besides, Athena asked almost the same question you did. It
can't do any harm, can it—my answering a simple question?

HERA

How much further?

HERMES

We're almost over Phrygia now. There's Ida—I can just make
out the peak of Gargarum, and if I'm not mistaken, there's Paris
right there.

HERA

Where? I can't see.

HERMES

Over there, to the left. No, not on top—down to the side, by that
cave where you see the herd.

HERA

I don't see the herd either.

APHRODITE

It's a good thing this isn't a "seeing" contest.

HERMES

Right there, between the rocks. Where I'm pointing, look—and the man running around with the staff, keeping them together …

HERA

Ah, I see now.

HERMES

Yes, that's him, all right. We should descend here—he might be frightened if we swoop down too suddenly.

HERA

Now that we're on the earth, Aphrodite, why don't you lead the way? I understand you've been here often enough to "visit" Anchises; or at least that's what I've heard.

APHRODITE

Your sneers are wasted on me, Hera.

HERMES

Come on, I'll lead the way myself. I spent enough time in the area while Zeus was courting Ganymede. Many times, I stood watch over the boy; and when the great eagle came and swooped him up, I flew at his side and helped with his lovely burden. I believe this is the very rock where he stood piping to his sheep as Zeus tenderly caught him up in those talons and carried the frightened boy off. I picked up his pipes, he had dropped them trying to escape, and—

HERA

Enough about my husband's philanderings.

HERMES

Oh, yes … sorry. Anyway, here is our appointed referee. Good morning, Paris!

PARIS

Hey, kid. Aren't you a little young to be climbing these
dangerous peaks? And with a band of women, no less!
Beautiful women—too beautiful for this mountain-side.

HERMES

These women, good Paris, are the Goddesses Hera, Athena, and
Aphrodite. And I am Hermes, messenger extraordinaire for
mighty Zeus. He has chosen you to judge the beauty of these
three, and the prize is this apple.

PARIS

An apple?

HERMES

I know, I know, but it's a very nice apple. And there's an
inscription. Here, have a look.

PARIS

"For the Fair." So, I ...

HERMES

Just give the apple to the fairest of the three. That's it. Couldn't
be simpler.

PARIS

But lord Hermes, how do you expect a mere goatherd to judge
between three such unparalleled beauties?

HERA

He speaks well, at least.

PARIS

Surely, there must be some fine city folk better suited to judge
this contest. I can tell you which of two goats is the finer beast,
or adjudicate the merits of two heifers, but in the present

company there is beauty all around. I don't know how any man could tear his eyes away from one to look on the other. Wherever my eyes fall—there is beauty. I move them, and what do I find—more loveliness! And yet I can't focus because I sense equal beauty lurking just this way or that! I am distracted by neighboring charms! If only I were all eyes, like Argus— then perhaps I could judge the matter!

APHRODITE
You're right, Hera—his speech is pretty.

HERMES
So it is. I'm sorry, Paris, but these are Zeus's orders—there's no way out of it. You are to decide the matter.

PARIS
All right, but the losers mustn't be angry with me. The fault will be with my eyes only—they are instruments far too crude for deciding such a fine matter.

HERMES
Zeus has already made this clear. There will be no retribution from the losing parties. Now get to work!

PARIS
All right, but … am I just to examine them as they are, or should I go into the matter more thoroughly?

HERMES
Well, that's for you to decide, I guess. Do whatever you think best.

PARIS
What I think best? Then I will be thorough.

HERMES

When you say "thorough" …

PARIS

I mean, if I'm to judge the entire package, perhaps they should disrobe.

HERMES

Disrobe?! You naughty boy! Do you really think—

HERA

Calm down, Hermes—the boy's quite right. I approve of your decision, Paris, and will be the first to submit myself to your inspection. You will find that I have more to boast of than white arms and large eyes—every part of me is beautiful.

PARIS

Aphrodite, will you also submit?

ATHENA

Oh, Paris—make sure she takes off that girdle; there's magic in it! She'll bewitch you! And she ought to wipe off all that makeup as well! She has no right to come so tricked out and painted!

APHRODITE

This is my natural hue.

HERA

Oh, please—you look like a prostitute.

APHRODITE

Excuse me?!

ATHENA

She really should show herself unadorned.

PARIS

The makeup can stay, but they're right about the girdle, madam—it must be removed.

APHRODITE

Oh, fine. But Athena has to take off her helmet then—no intimidating the judge with that waving plume. Or are you afraid your colorless eyes might be exposed without their formidable surroundings?

ATHENA

I'm afraid of no such thing. Here is my helmet.

APHRODITE

And here is my girdle.

HERA

Good. Let's get on with it.

PARIS

God of wonders! What beauty is here! Oh, rapture! How exquisite these ladies' charms! How dazzling the majesty of Heaven's true queen! And oh, how sweet, how captivating is Aphrodite's smile! And Athena's taut muscles! It's too much! I'm overwhelmed by your combined beauty! I know not where to look! My eyes are drawn all ways at once—they're splitting apart!

APHRODITE

Perhaps he should view us one at a time.

HERA

Yes, we don't want the poor boy's eyes to explode.

HERMES

All right, then—Aphrodite, you and Athena withdraw with me. Let Hera remain.

APHRODITE

So be it.

[APHRODITE, ATHENA, and HERMES withdraw.]

HERA

Well, do you like what you see?

PARIS

Words cannot express my satisfaction, madam.

HERA

When you have finished your scrutiny, you must decide how you would like your present.

PARIS

My present?

HERA

That's right. Give me the prize of beauty, Paris, and I will make you lord of all Asia!

PARIS

I will take no presents, madam. Withdraw, and I shall judge as I see fit.

[HERA withdraws.]

Approach, Athena.

ATHENA

Behold.

PARIS
You are very beautiful.

ATHENA
If you will crown me the fairest, Paris, I will make you a great warrior—a conquering hero! I will cast a divine spell so that you will never lose a battle!

PARIS
I appreciate the offer, Athena—but I'm a lover, not a fighter. There's peace throughout the land, and my father's rule is uncontested. What use do I have for fighting? You can put your robe back on, and your helmet; I've seen enough.
          [ATHENA exits.]
And now for Aphrodite.

APHRODITE
Here I am. Take your time, and examine every inch as carefully as you like; let nothing escape your vigilance. Don't be shy. Put your hand here. There, now that's better—isn't it? You're a handsome boy, Paris—I've had my eye on you for a long time. You must be the fairest youth in all of Phrygia. It's such a pity that you're hidden away in these rocks and crags. Your beauty is wasted on these goats. I'd like to whisk you away and marry you to some Greek girl—an Argive, or Corinthian, or maybe a Spartan, if you like a girl with a little spunk. Helen is a Spartan. Such a pretty girl—quite as pretty as I am.

PARIS
As pretty as you?

APHRODITE
Oh, yes. And such a lover of beauty. I'm quite certain, if she once caught sight of you, she would give up everything to be with you. She would make a most devoted wife.

PARIS

But … I'm already married.

APHRODITE

So is she. But that's of no importance. When marriage exists without love, such bonds are easily broken.

PARIS

Tell me about her—this Helen.

APHRODITE

Well, she's the daughter of Leda—you know, the beauty Zeus ravaged in the guise of a swan.

PARIS

And what is she like?

APHRODITE

Helen is the fairest of the fair, and as one might expect from the offspring of the swan, she is soft as down (she was hatched from an egg, you know), and so lithe and graceful; her figure is the picture of perfection. She's already had one war fought over her after she was abducted by Theseus—and she was just a child then. Now she's all grown up and married to Menelaus, but if you'd like, I will make her your wife.

PARIS

Won't Menelaus be angry?

APHRODITE

Don't worry about the details, child; I'll protect you.

PARIS

I don't want to cause any problems.

APHRODITE

No problem at all. I will arrange to have you set out for Greece on a little vacation. When you get to Sparta, Helen won't be able to resist your charms.

PARIS

But … will she really leave her husband and cross the seas with a complete stranger? A goatherd?

APHRODITE

Trust me. I have two beautiful children, Love and Desire—they shall be your guides.

PARIS

I don't know how this will end, but I feel like I'm in love with Helen already. I can see her in my mind, on our homeward journey from Sparta, her hand wrapped in mine as we stare across the sea.

APHRODITE

Wait! Don't fall in love yet. There's still the little matter of crowning me the most beautiful of the Goddesses. Eternal happiness is yours—all you have to do is hand me that apple.

PARIS

Are you sure you won't forget me after I give you the prize?

APHRODITE

Shall I swear?

PARIS

No; your word is enough.

APHRODITE

You shall have Helen for your wife; she shall follow you and make Troy her home—this I promise.

PARIS
Take the apple. It's yours.

XXI

Ares. Hermes.

ARES

Hermes! Did you hear Zeus storming? He was in quite a rage.
"If the whim strikes me," he said, "I could hang a cord from
Heaven with all of you dangling from it, and your combined
weight couldn't pull me down! On the other hand, if I chose to
haul you up, with earth and sea in the bargain, I wouldn't even
break a sweat!" I dare say, it's empty boasting on his part. Of
course he's too much for any of us individually, but I refuse to
believe we couldn't take him if we combined our efforts.

HERMES

Be careful what you say, Ares—it isn't safe to talk like that.

ARES

I wouldn't risk this talk with just anyone, Hermes, but I know
you can keep quiet. I have to say though, it made me laugh the
way he stormed about and flashed his thunderbolts. I couldn't
help but get the feeling he was putting on a show out of fear we
might actually gang up on him. I remember not long ago he was
frightened out of his wits when Poseidon, Hera, and Athena
rebelled and tried to imprison him. They would have succeeded,
too, if Thetis hadn't intervened and sent the hundred-handed
monster Briareus to save him. You have to admit, the thought of
Zeus in chains is rather amusing.

HERMES

Shut up! If you want to talk about this, you'll have to find
someone else to listen—it's too dangerous!

XXII

Pan. Hermes.

PAN

Hello, father.

HERMES

What are you talking about? I'm not your father.

PAN

Aren't you Hermes?

HERMES

Sure—who are you?

PAN

I'm your son—the result of an irregular intrigue.

HERMES

An intrigue of goats maybe! How could you be mine with your horns and cloven feet and that tail on your ass?

PAN

If you sneer at me, it is your own son you make the object of reproach, and by association, yourself, since you're responsible for begetting me. I'm just an innocent product of your overactive libido.

HERMES

All right, then. If I'm your father, who is your mother? Did I accidentally fall upon some she-goat in the barnyard?

PAN

You mock me, but think hard and see if you can't remember taking a gentle Arcadian girl against her will. Why do you bite your thumb to find an answer? It's not a difficult question. I'm talking, of course, about Penelope, the daughter of Icarus.

HERMES

If that's true, then why do you resemble a goat more than your own father?

PAN

That's a question I've asked myself more than once. After putting me off for years, she finally admitted that, at the time of your union, you had taken the form of a goat to avoid detection, and for that reason I am cursed to walk the earth with horns and cloven feet and a tail on my ass.

HERMES

I have to admit, your story does ring a bell, although I can't quite recall the details. Still, do you expect me, a God who prides himself on his striking good looks, to have the reputation of fathering such a ridiculous-looking creature?

PAN

I won't disgrace you, father. I'm a musician.

HERMES

Oh, what do you play?

PAN

The pipes. I've earned quite a reputation in musical circles. And I just scored a sweet gig with Bacchus, leading the dance for him.

HERMES

A musician? That's fine for entertaining, but it's hardly a respectable profession.

PAN

I've got other assets as well. You should see my flocks—they're so numerous they stretch from Epidaurus to the Ionian Sea.

HERMES

A real man wouldn't be caught dead tending flocks—he would be out making a name for himself on the battlefield!

PAN

I distinguished myself so much at Marathon, fighting for the Athenians, that I was awarded a prize of valor—the cave under the Acropolis. If you go to Athens, you will see how respected is the name of Pan!

HERMES

Pan? Ah, yes, I've heard of you. But tell me, are you married?

PAN

Never! I have a healthy libido myself and could never be satisfied with just one wife.

HERMES

No doubt you've made love to many she-goats.

PAN

Is that supposed to be funny? I've indulged myself with many beautiful women, including Echo and Pitys and all the Maenads of Bacchus. And they certainly haven't complained.

HERMES

That's my boy! But listen, do me one favor …

PAN

Anything, father.

HERMES

Come give me a hug, but let's keep this whole affair between the two of us, all right? I'll gladly accept you as my son as long as you promise not to tell anyone about it.

XXIII

Apollo. Dionysus.

APOLLO
Are we really expected to believe that Eros, Hermaphroditus, and Priapus come from the same mother? They're nothing alike! One is a handsome and powerful ruler; the second is effeminate to the point of ambiguousness—you can't even tell if he's a young man or a virgin; and the third is masculine beyond all bounds of decency—Priapus, I mean.

DIONYSUS
There's really nothing surprising about it, Apollo. The differences come not from Aphrodite, but from the three different fathers. Even when children are by the same father, the often develop very differently. Take you and your sister, for instance.

APOLLO
We're very similar—we're both archers.

DIONYSUS
Sure, but that's where the similarities end. You've become a prophet and a doctor, while Artemis murders strangers among the Scythians.

APOLLO
She only does that out of necessity. Don't you think if any Greek ever happened upon the Tauric peninsula, she'd gladly sail away with him and abandon her sacrificial butchery.

DIONYSUS
Maybe this particular example hits too close to home. As for Priapus, however, let me tell you something which may alter

your opinion. I recently travelled through Lampsacus, where he
played the role of host and took me in as an honored guest.
After dinner, I retired to rest and ... somewhere around
midnight, my excellent host ... I blush to tell you.

APOLLO

Did he make an attempt on your virtue, Dionysus?

DIONYSUS

A rather energetic attempt.

APOLLO

What did you do?

DIONYSUS

What could I do? I laughed at him.

APOLLO

Well done! Of course, Priapus is to be excused for this
particular lapse in judgment, considering that his attempt was
directed at such a good-looking youth as yourself.

DIONYSUS

For that same reason, my dear Apollo, he might direct similar
attention your way; for you are also an attractive youth with
your long flowing tresses. He might attempt your virtue even in
his sober moments.

APOLLO

I doubt that, Dionysus; for, with my flowing hair, I have sharp
arrows, also.

XXIV

Hermes. Maia.

HERMES
I'm going to kill myself.

MAIA
Don't say such things, child.

HERMES
It isn't fair! Why do I have to be the whipping boy? I'm a God just like the rest of them, but it's always "Hermes! Do this! Hermes! Do that!" I'm surprised they haven't started tipping me! I might as well be a servant! I get all the grunt work, the mindless labor, and I never say a word! I get up early, sweep the kitchen, lay out all the cushions so Zeus can be nice and comfy—then I spend the whole day rushing his messages back and forth, up and down! No sooner am I finished with that (no time for a bath) then I have to set the table and make sure all the forks are in their proper place—before this new cup-bearer came I had to pour the nectar too! And afterwards, while everyone else is letting their food settle and enjoying pleasant conversation, I'm off to Pluto with the Shades, to play the usher in Rhadamanthus's court! It's not enough that I'm busy all day delivering Zeus's proclamations in the wrestling arena and the Assembly and the schools of rhetoric—the dead must have their share of me too! Leda's sons take turns alternating between Heaven and Hades—I have to be in both at once! And why should the mortals among us feast as they please, while I—the son of Maia, the grandson of Atlas—wait upon them hand and foot?! Here I am just back from Sidon, where he sent me to check on Europa, and before I can even catch my breath again, I'm off to Argos in quest of Danae! "And oh, by the way," he

says, "Can you stop in Boeotia and drop this note to Antiope?" I might as well just kill myself before I drop dead from exhaustion! Mortal slaves are better off than I am—at least they have some hope of being sold to a new master!

MAIA

Come, come, child. Be a good boy and do what your father asks—run along to Argos and Boeotia, and stop wasting time with this silly talk, or you really will get a whipping. Lovers, you know, are apt to be hasty.

XXV

Zeus. Helios.

ZEUS

What the hell were you thinking?! How could you trust your
chariot to a silly boy like that?! He almost destroyed the whole
planet, coming too near and scorching the earth in some places,
and in others killing everything with frost by pulling too far
away! If I hadn't been there with my thunderbolt to see what
was happening, all of mankind would have been destroyed!

HELIOS

I made a mistake, Zeus. I was wrong. But don't treat me with
too much contempt, he was my son. And there's no way I could
have known it would turn out like this.

ZEUS

Oh, no—of course not. You had no idea what a delicate
business this is, how the slightest error could put the entire
planet in peril! I'm sure you never realized how spirited the
horses are, or what a strong hand it takes to keep them in line!
You had no idea they would lead him by the nose this way and
that, now right, now left, now completely backwards, and up or
down, just as their whims suggested! There might as well have
been no driver at all!

HELIOS

I know—you're right. I knew it would happen. That's why I
held out as long as I did. But he begged and wept, and his
mother nagged me mercilessly, and he was my son after all—I
wanted him to succeed. I showed him how to hold the reins,
how to stand, when to descend and when to mount upwards. I
demonstrated how to keep the beasts under control. I explained
how dangerous it was if he didn't keep the track. And finally, he

convinced me he could do it. But when he found himself in
charge of all that fire, and staring down into yawning space, he
got scared, and the horses sensed it right away. The sized him
up and left the track, wrought all the havoc you've described,
and my poor boy let go the reins—he thought he was going to be
thrown out, I suspect—and held on to the rail. But he has paid
the ultimate price for his mistake, and there is no punishment
you can deal to me greater than my grief.

ZEUS

You've brought this upon yourself, Helios. You should have
known better. I'll forgive you this time, but if anything like this
ever happens again, you will feel the sting of my thunderbolt
yourself. Let his sisters bury him by the Eridanus—their grief
shall change them into poplars so that no one shall ever forget
what has happened here today.

HELIOS

Must I lose more of my children?

ZEUS

Be grateful this is the only concession I ask of you! Now get to
your chariot—the pole is broken, and one of the wheels is
crushed—make the necessary repairs and drive the route
yourself. Quickly, before I change my mind.

XXVI

Apollo. Hermes.

APOLLO
Hermes, how do you tell them apart?

HERMES
Who?

APOLLO
Castor and Pollux—I can't tell which is which.

HERMES
Yesterday was Castor, and today is Pollux.

APOLLO
But how do you tell? They're exactly alike!

HERMES
If you look closely, Pollux's face is scarred from that boxing match with Amycus, the Bebrycian. Castor has no marks at all—his face is still perfect.

APOLLO
Ah! Thanks! It's always so embarrassing when I don't know what name to use—I'm always calling Pollux "Castor," and Castor "Pollux." Why is it, by the way, that they're never here together? Why do they alternate between gods and shades?

HERMES
That's their brotherly way. It was decreed that one of the sons of Leda must die, and the other be immortal—so they came up with this equitable arrangement by which they split the immortality between them.

82

APOLLO

It seems a rather strange way of doing it. If one of them must be in Heaven while the other is underground, they will be separated for all eternity.

HERMES

Better that than permanent death for one of them, I suppose.

APOLLO

They have plenty of time for work, I guess. What is their profession by the way? All the other gods have some sort of business they practice. I'm a prophet, Asclepius is a doctor, Artemis serves as midwife—what are these two going to do? I assume they won't just sit around all day?

HERMES

Oh no. Their business is to patrol the ocean—if they see a ship in trouble, they board her and save the crew.

APOLLO

A worthy profession.

* * *

LaVergne, TN USA
11 August 2010
192905LV00004B/31/P